ANASTASIA MORNINGSTAR

Sarah, alone on the steps, frowned and pocketed her notebook. She looked around the yard, under the steps, and along the house. Her eyes caught for a moment a flash of clear light near the flowers, but it was quickly gone. Then, on the step behind her, Sarah saw the small, carved bird which Anna had been working on. It looked to Sarah like a sea gull, one of the freewheeling gulls that sailed high above the playing grounds down by the river. She reached over and picked it up.

Instantly she was in the air high above the city. Below her was the river and the park and the maze of streets and houses that stretched out for miles. The wind was sleek against her feathers. Feathers! She was a bird!

"Charmingly written and peopled with winning characters, this tale successfully combines realism with fantasy to produce a celebration of the wonders of the natural world . . . An enchanting story for transitional readers."

—*School Library Journal*

Anastasia Morningstar

HAZEL HUTCHINS
Illustrated by Julie Tennent

PUFFIN BOOKS

PUFFIN BOOKS
Published by the Penguin Group
Viking Penguin, a division of Penguin Books USA Inc.,
375 Hudson Street, New York, New York 10014, U.S.A.
Penguin Books Ltd, 27 Wrights Lane, London W8 5TZ, England
Penguin Books Australia Ltd, Ringwood, Victoria, Australia
Penguin Books Canada Ltd, 10 Alcorn Avenue, Toronto, Ontario, Canada M4V 3B2
Penguin Books (N.Z.) Ltd, 182–190 Wairau Road, Auckland 10, New Zealand

Penguin Books Ltd, Registered Offices: Harmondsworth, Middlesex, England

First published in Canada as *Anastasia Morningstar and the Crystal
Butterfly* by Annick Press Ltd., 1984
First published in Great Britain with illustrations
by Julie Tennent by Penguin Books Ltd., 1989
First published in the United States of America
by Viking Penguin, a division of Penguin Books USA Inc, 1990
Published in Puffin Books, 1992
1 3 5 7 9 10 8 6 4 2
Text copyright © Hazel Hutchins, 1984
Illustrations copyright © Julie Tennent, 1989
All rights reserved

LIBRARY OF CONGRESS CATALOGING-IN-PUBLICATION DATA
Hutchins, H. J. (Hazel J.)
[Anastasia Morningstar and the crystal butterfly]
Anastasia Morningstar / by Hazel Hutchins ; illustrated by Julie
Tennent.   p. cm.
"First published in Canada as Anastasia Morningstar and the
crystal butterfly . . . 1984"—CIP verso t.p.
Summary: When Sarah and Ben meet the mysterious and intriguing
Anastasia Morningstar, they decide that her uncanny magical powers
would be the perfect subject for their science project.
ISBN 0-14-034343-1
[1. Magic—Fiction.   2. Science projects—Fiction.]   I. Tennent,
Julie, ill.   II. Title.
PZ7.H96162An   1992   [Fic]—dc20   91-31747

Printed in the United States of America
Set in Aldus

But when the light begins with age
To dull and wax upon its wings,
One will come with spirit strong
Therein light of renewal sings.
In search of sun and wind and sky
Three shall gather, high on high,
To free the crystal butterfly.

Anastasia Morningstar

CHAPTER ONE

On a bright morning in May the lady at the corner grocery store turned Derek Henshaw into a frog.

It happened very quietly. In fact, if Sarah and Ben hadn't been in the store looking for macaroni for their science project, and if they hadn't been watching Derek to see what he was going to steal (he always stole something), no one—except Derek and the woman—would have known what happened.

But they were there. They saw it all from behind the rack of potato chips. Derek slipped a water pistol into his pocket. A hand reached out from around the corner and touched him on the left shoulder. A voice spoke a single word.

"Frog."

Derek was gone. On the floor in the middle of the aisle was a frog. The frog blinked once, croaked twice, and hopped out the open door. The woman who worked at the store smiled to herself all the way back to the cash register.

Ben looked at Sarah and Sarah looked at Ben. Of one mind, they ducked low. They crept behind the potato chips and around a large stack of toilet paper to where they could see through the front windows of the store.

Derek Henshaw was sitting on the curb in front of the store. He looked two shades sneakier and tougher and even more bad-tempered than he usually did, but he was no longer a frog. The only thing at all peculiar about him, in fact, was the way he was sitting with his large knobbly knees up around his ears.

As Sarah and Ben watched, first one leg and then the other slipped down into a normal position. He spotted Sarah and Ben watching him from behind the windows. He scowled at them, but he did not come back into the store. Instead, he turned and walked away down the street. And although one

4

could tell he was trying to walk in a perfectly normal way, there was the oddest hitch to his step; a small, half-stifled jerk that had faded, but still had not gone completely, when he finally passed from view.

"That's it," whispered Ben. "I'm leaving."

He and Sarah stole down the aisle, out the door, and around the corner of the building.

"Wait," called Sarah as they reached the alley.

Ben stopped and looked at Sarah. Sarah crept back to the edge of the building and peered around the corner.

Through the windows Sarah could see the woman who worked behind the counter of the store. She was filling the slush machine. Sarah had

seen her countless times before but this time she looked at her with renewed interest.

She was a perfectly normal-looking woman: not too tall and not too short with dark eyes and long dark hair that she wore braided and pinned neatly around her head. If her hair had been short and her eyes not quite so dark she would have looked a good deal like Sarah's Aunt Em, except that Sarah's Aunt Em didn't go around turning people into frogs. Not that Sarah knew of, at least.

Sarah knew the woman's name. She had heard it spoken once in the store and she had remembered it. It was a rather grand name for someone who looked so ordinary. Her name was Anastasia Morningstar.

*   *   *

Sarah Mathews and Ben Clark lived across the street from each other. Sarah lived with her mother. Ben lived with his mother, his father, three brothers, one sister, Grandpa Butler, two dogs, three budgies, and a cousin who came and went from time to time. When Sarah wanted to liven up her day she went over to Ben's house. When Ben needed a little peace and quiet, he went over to Sarah's house. They both had other good friends but, all in all, Sarah and Ben understood each other. That was why Ben knew, without needing to ask, that Sarah was thinking very, very hard as they walked home together. Sarah thought very hard about a good number of things. It was a little frightening at times.

"I think she did it by mass hypnosis," said Ben at last as they rounded the corner onto their street.

Sarah looked at Ben and frowned.

"Either that or she used mirrors," said Ben.

Sarah frowned even harder.

"In any case," said Ben, "I think we should both keep out of Derek's way for about two years, just in case he thinks we had something to do with it."

"Something to do with what?" asked Sarah.

"You know," said Ben. "It."

"It what?" asked Sarah.

Ben looked over his shoulder to make sure no one could hear them.

"Derek being turned into a frog!" said Ben.

Sarah looked at Ben and smiled. It was not a very big smile. It was just big enough to show exactly how she felt.

"I don't think it was mass hypnosis or mirrors either," she said. "I think she really turned him into a frog."

"But how could she do it?" demanded Ben.

"I don't know," said Sarah. "But she did."

"She'd have to be really, really weird," said Ben. "I mean *really* weird."

"I know," said Sarah. "In fact, she's perfect."

"Perfect?" asked Ben.

"For my science project," said Sarah.

Ben's eyebrows dropped low over his eyes.

"We're doing a macaroni moonscape complete with a scale model of a futuristic solar-powered lunar station," said Ben.

"*You're* doing a moonscape," said Sarah. "It was your idea in the first place. The only reason you let me in on it was because Mr. Wyanth wanted you to. He thinks I can't find anything good to do on my own. Well, I just have."

Ben didn't answer. What Sarah had said was true.

They were standing now in front of Ben's house. Through the screen door they could hear the usual tumult of voices within. Sarah sat on the front steps. Ben slipped inside and reappeared with an apple in each hand. He tossed one to Sarah.

"Mr. Wyanth isn't going to like this," said Ben matter-of-factly. "You know how he is about science. He likes it straight: no talking animals, no incredible super-heroes. I've a feeling that what you're getting into is worse than either."

"I'll handle Mr. Wyanth," said Sarah. "But will you help me at least, Ben? I might, you know, need help."

Ben knew exactly what Sarah meant. He looked around him at the nice, normal, dependable world

where everything happened, if not exactly orderly, at least according to certain reliable expectations.

"I still have to work on my moonscape," said Ben.

"I'll help," said Sarah. "I'll do everything exactly the way you tell me to. I won't disagree with anything, and I won't make any suggestions, and I won't change things when you're not looking."

This sounded very fine to Ben. There was, however, still something bothering him.

"I don't particularly want to be known as the school crazy either," said Ben.

"Neither do I," said Sarah. "That's why we're not going to tell anybody except Mr. Wyanth. Mr. Wyanth doesn't think much of me, you know. He says he's going to flunk me in science if my project isn't any good. Well, this year my project is going to be more than good. It's going to more like amazing." Sarah smiled to herself. "Now, will you help me?"

Ben looked around him one last time. Everything on the street looked perfectly, predictably normal and, frankly, just a shade dull.

"OK," he said. "I'll help. When do we start?"

CHAPTER TWO

Andrew Wyanth taught science to grades four, five, and six. His science room was in the basement of John Diefenbaker Elementary School. The front of the room was very much like an average classroom. The back of the room, depending on the time of the year, could be a three-dimensional solar system, a prehistoric dinosaur landscape, a weather station, a chemistry lab, or a mock-up atom. It was always a zoo. Three tanks of fish, two snakes, and several chameleons lived permanently on the premises. Occasional rabbits, guinea pigs, frogs, pupating insects, ant colonies—in fact, anything that could fit in a small area—sooner or later found its way to the back of the classroom.

The animals sometimes escaped. Mr. Wyanth was rescuing a snake that had wound its way around the wire orbit that pierced the planet Mars when Sarah and Ben found him at noon the next day. The snake was distinctly peeved. Mr. Wyanth was not in a very good mood either.

"Please," he said, putting the snake back in its warm, safe terrarium. "Please, Sarah Mathews, tell me you're not here with another proposal for what you want to do for your science project."

"This one's good," said Sarah.

Mr. Wyanth looked hard at Sarah. Then he turned to Ben.

"I thought you two were going to do a moon-scape," he said.

"I still am," said Ben. "This is Sarah's project, not mine."

"I see," said Mr. Wyanth. He sighed and sat down on top of the nearest desk. Sarah's projects generally took a while to explain. This time, how-ever, the whole project came out in one phrase.

"Necromancy: Fact or Fiction," said Sarah.

"Necromancy?" repeated Mr. Wyanth.

"Necromancy," said Sarah. "It's a fancy word for black magic."

"I know what it means," said Mr. Wyanth. "What I don't know is how on earth it relates to science, unless you're trying to set us back about three hundred years."

"Suppose," said Sarah, "just suppose, there was a lady working down at some corner grocery store somewhere who could turn people into frogs. Wouldn't she be of interest to the scientific com-munity as an as yet not fully investigated scientific phenomenon?"

Mr. Wyanth looked at Ben.

"Do you understand what she's talking about?" he asked.

"I'm doing a macaroni moonscape, complete with a matchstick model of a futuristic lunar space station," said Ben, and he set his lips together very

13

tightly in a manner that clearly indicated he wasn't going to explain anything further.

Mr. Wyanth looked at Sarah and sighed. He'd had a particularly hard morning. First he'd had to clean up after the parrot. Then he'd found Derek Henshaw, who was in the grade higher than Sarah and Ben, poking at the frogs in the aquarium and trying to feed them cigarette butts. Then the snake. And now Sarah. Sarah. Every class had someone like Sarah in it, someone who couldn't quite keep to the straight path, but Sarah was worse than most. In science it was important to keep to the straight and logical path. The more Mr. Wyanth pointed out to Sarah that she was in danger of flunking science because of her failure to realize this fact, the wilder her schemes became.

It occurred to Andrew Wyanth, this morning, that it was no longer any use trying to guide Sarah through calmer channels. Better just to let her run amuck.

"That will be fine, Sarah," he said. "But remember, I want to preview all the projects next week."

"I'll remember," said Sarah. "Thank you, Mr. Wyanth."

Ben and Sarah walked out into the hall. It was almost time for class and there was a steady flow of students up and down the corridors.

"I can't believe he went for it that easily," said

Sarah. "I had a whole bunch of arguments to confuse him with."

"He hasn't gone for it at all," said Ben. "He doesn't believe a word you said."

"Remember to meet me after school outside the store," said Sarah.

"I'll remember," said Ben. "But I wish you had more of a plan."

"I've got lots of plans," said Sarah. "I just don't know which one is the right one yet."

*   *   *

Anastasia Morningstar was fired that afternoon from her job at the corner grocery store. She had been fired before, so it was not new to her, but it hurt nonetheless.

As usual, the owner of the store had told Anna he was sorry to let her go. Several good things had happened since she had arrived. The place was perfectly clean. The money in the cash register always came out right. The shoplifting that had once gone on at an alarming rate had stopped entirely. True, there had been a few unusual complaints, but when the owner had asked people to be more specific, they had always backed down.

Mr. Henshaw, however, had not backed down. He had not bothered to explain, but he hadn't backed down either. Mr. Henshaw was the manager at the bank where the store owed money.

Anastasia agreed to leave without arguing. She took her check and the basket of fruit that the owner had given her as a goodwill gesture and she left for good at the end of her afternoon shift.

She was sad. When she got to the park she stopped and sat quietly among the trees for a long time, feeling the strength of their living wood and the touch of wind and sunlight among their leaves overhead. When she felt a little better she walked home. It was only as she turned onto her street that she became aware that Sarah and Ben were watching her every step of the way.

Anna's house was on Twenty-third Street, three blocks past the park. It was a small, older house in a row of small, older houses. It was blue with white shutters, that had not been meant for shutting, and a white crisscross latticed window on the front— the kind that looks truly homey at Christmas when you spray the corners with artificial snow.

Anna walked in the front door, through the house, and, very quietly, out the back door. She found Sarah and Ben in the honeysuckle bush beneath the side window. They were peering inexpertly through the pane. She touched each of them with one finger on their left shoulder and spoke a single word.

"Stone."

Two stones appeared under the honeysuckle

bush where the children's feet had stood. They were smooth and gray and rounded. Anna picked up one and then the other. Cradling them in her arms, she carried them back to the park and set them beneath some bushes. Then she walked home again.

CHAPTER THREE

Stones do not think, but they do have a good deal of atmosphere about them. A stone has eons and eons of time to pass before it is ground down by wind and water into the sands that eventually find their way to the bottom of the sea. A stone spans the centuries in a way that a human life cannot. Sarah felt it. Ben felt it. The feeling was still with them when they became human again, crouched beneath some bushes in the middle of the park.

Even when they could feel their living, breathing bodies, neither Sarah nor Ben moved or spoke for some time. They were unwilling to break from that different state of being while it still lingered close and real within them.

At last Sarah stretched out her legs. Ben uncurled and lay long on the soft grass.

"What do you think?" asked Sarah.

"I don't think she likes being snooped on," said Ben.

"That's what I think," said Sarah. "We'll have to take a more direct approach."

Dear Anastasia Morningstar,

My friend Ben and I are sorry for peering in the window of your house. It is my fault actually because I'm the one who is flunking science. Could you be my science project for Mr. Wyanth's class at school? The title of my project is Necromancy: Fact or Fiction. *I don't know exactly what you have in your repertoire—but a few frogs would do just fine.*

Yours truly,
Sarah Mathews

P.S. We'll call back after school to arrange details with you then.

Sarah left the note on Anna's front door at noon the next day. When she and Ben returned, there was a package on the front step. On the package was written in neat letters: "For Sarah Mathews from Anastasia Morningstar."

Sarah and Ben took the package back to Sarah's house. They unwrapped it on the kitchen table. It was a small box, 10 inches high and 10 inches wide. It was made of wood. A flowered design had been painted on it carefully by hand. At one corner a butterfly was painted—a butterfly with wings as clear as glass.

"What's in it?" asked Ben.

Sarah opened the box. Inside was a robin's egg. Once she and her father had scrambled up on top of an old shed and looked down into a nest with three such lovely blue eggs. Sarah looked at it, then closed the box and handed it across to Ben.

Ben opened the box.

"Hey!" he said. "A dot nickel!"

"What?" asked Sarah.

"A 1947 dot nickel! I had one once! They're not

worth a whole lot of money like a dot penny but they're pretty rare. Grandpa used mine to buy a paper. I never did tell him what he'd done but I could hardly look at him for a whole month without feeling sick about it."

"Let me see," said Sarah.

She took the box. Inside was a small blue robin's egg.

"I see a robin's egg," she said.

"I see a dot nickel," said Ben.

Ben looked at Sarah and Sarah looked at Ben.

"Let's go ask your mom what she sees," said Ben.

Sarah's mom was mowing the lawn out back. She turned off the mower when she saw Sarah and Ben.

"That's a lovely box," she said.

"There's something inside," said Ben. "But we're not sure what it is."

Sarah's mother opened the box and smiled.

"It's a clan brooch," she said. "In fact, it's a McLean clan brooch. My mother, your grand-mother, Sarah, was a McLean. She had a brooch just like this. Where did you find it?"

"The lady at the corner store gave it to me," said Sarah. "The lady with the dark hair done up in braids. I told her I needed a science project and she gave me this."

"Well, I don't know what it's got to do with a science project but it's lovely, really lovely." Sarah's mother took one last look and sighed. "I think you'd better give it back to her, Sarah."

"But she gave it to me," said Sarah.

"Did she really? Or did she just want to let you borrow it? It seems to me something she must be very fond of. I think you should take it back and talk to her about it before it gets lost or broken. Things like this mean a lot to people."

Sarah's mother sighed and closed the box.

"Do I have to?" asked Sarah.

"Yes," said her mother. "Put it somewhere safe for tonight and return it tomorrow on your way home from school at noon."

"We blew it," said Sarah as she and Ben went back into the house.

"Maybe your mother is right," said Ben. "She doesn't really know about the box but maybe she's right. A box like this would mean a lot to someone. Why would she give it to us anyway?" Sarah shrugged.

"Maybe she liked my letter," she said. "I write a pretty good letter, you know. Anyway, I think it means we'll be safe enough if we take it back to her at the store. She won't, you know, turn us into anything."

Anastasia Morningstar, of course, was not at the store the next day at noon. Sarah and Ben took the box back to her house. She did not answer the door, so they left it on the front step where they had found it. Sarah wrote another note:

Dear Anastasia Morningstar,

Thank you for the box. My mother says it is much too lovely and must mean a lot to you and I have to give it back. I don't think it would really work as a science project, anyway. Just in case you're interested, here is what the people we showed it to saw inside.

Sarah (me)	robin's egg
Ben	1947 dot nickel
My mom	McLean clan brooch
Ben's older brother	Swiss Army officer's knife
Derek (the frog) Henshaw	black widow spider (We had Ben's brother show him the box for us.)
Mr. Serra at the store	one hundred Italian lire
Mr. Wyanth (Science teacher)	butterfly

Mr. Serra at the store told us you didn't work there anymore. We told him that if it was because of anything Derek Henshaw had said or done, he shouldn't believe it because we saw Derek steal the *water pistol and he's been ripping off the store for a long time.*

Yours truly,
Sarah Mathews

P.S. Are you sure you wouldn't like to be part of my science project? It would only take a moment of your time. Please.

CHAPTER FOUR

Anastasia Morningstar was sitting on the front steps of her house when Sarah and Ben went to visit her three days later. She was carving a bird in flight out of a piece of light-colored wood. The head and wings were smooth and perfect. The tail was slowly finding its shape out of the roughness of wood that had been prepared for it. She set it gently aside as Ben and Sarah approached.

"Hi," said Sarah. "I'm Sarah and this is Ben. Thanks for inviting us over."

"It was getting rather hard, talking by letter all the time," said Anastasia Morningstar. "You can call me Anna, if you like."

"Good," said Sarah. She sat down on the step beside Anna. "Do I start or do you?"

"I don't know," said Anna. "How do you start?"

Sarah took a small notepad and a pencil from her hip pocket.

"I've got some questions," she said. "Number one, how did you learn to do what you do?"

"Let's try question number two," said Anna.

"Number two, do you belong to a group or a coven or something neat like that?"

"Let's try number three," said Anna.

"How long have you been turning people into frogs?" asked Sarah.

"Interesting questions," said Anna. "I think we'll have a break for tea. Everything is ready in the kitchen to bring out."

Anna stood up.

"I'll help," said Ben. He followed her into the house.

Sarah, alone on the steps, frowned and pocketed her notebook. She looked around the yard, under the steps and along the house. Her eyes caught for a moment a flash of clear light near the flowers, but it was quickly gone. Then, on the step behind her, Sarah saw the small, carved bird which Anna had been working on. It looked to Sarah like a sea gull, one of the freewheeling gulls that sailed high above the playing grounds down by the river. She reached over and picked it up.

Instantly she was in the air high above the city. Below her was the river and the park and the maze of streets and houses that stretched out for miles. The wind was sleek against her feathers. Feathers! She was a bird!

She was circling, turning slowly on the air cur-

rents themselves. She could feel their buoyancy. She could almost taste their texture. Her eyes were sharp and clear. She picked out her own house, and the school, and the street where Anna lived. She let the air carry her soaring toward them. The currents lifted her, lifted her.

Then it happened. The air dropped beneath her. Instinctively, she swept her wings downward. Again and again she pushed with her wings but she was falling. She beat her wings harder. It was something else. Something else was wrong. She began to spiral awkwardly downward. Desperately she tried to steer for Anna's house. She was falling hard and fast now. She began calling, calling, screaming in her high, urgent, gull's voice as the air rushed from beneath her and her wings failed over and over and over again.

"Sarah!"

Sarah Mathews was sitting on the steps of Anastasia Morningstar's front porch. Anna was standing beside her, holding the carved bird in the palm of her hand.

"Are you all right?"

Sarah thought for a moment. Toes, fingers, knees, heartbeat. . . .

"Fine," she said.

"Good," said Anna. "You should have let go of the carving. It wasn't meant for you in the first place."

"Don't give it to anyone you like," Sarah said. "It's defective."

Anna frowned. Then she seemed to understand. She turned the bird and held it by the beak to show the still-unformed tail.

"You were flying without a proper stabilizer," she said.

"That explains it," said Sarah.

"Maybe we should have tea in the house," said Anna.

"Right," said Sarah. She followed Anna inside.

There was Chinese tea and thick slices of banana bread on the kitchen table. If it had been something noisier to eat than banana bread it would have been

embarrassing because no one talked while they were eating. Sarah seemed to be thinking very hard. Once or twice she opened her mouth, but she always shut it again without actually saying anything. The only sound, for a long time, was the muffled slurp of carefully sipped tea. Then Anna swept her arm lightly across the table, as if to gather up the crumbs. Beneath her hand the table turned crystal clear and alive with a moving hue of rainbow colors in its depths.

"How do you do it?" Ben asked breathlessly.

Anna smiled.

"I just do it," she said. "Do you like it?"

"Yes," said Ben.

"You could be famous," said Sarah. "You would be wonderful on TV or in a grand New York magic show!"

Anna shook her head.

"Those things are for people who do magic," she said.

"But *you* do magic," said Sarah. "Except that it's real."

"Real magic?" asked Anna.

"If it's real," said Ben, and then he stopped to think a moment, "then it can't be magic. At least not exactly. I mean, in one way it can. But in another way, it can't."

Sarah frowned.

"But *you* do it?" she asked.

"Oh yes," said Anna smiling. She swept her hand back over the table and returned it to normal.

"Good," said Sarah. "And you are going to be my science project, aren't you? That's why you invited us here, isn't it?"

"I'd like to do something for you," said Anna. "After you talked to Mr. Serra at the store, he dug a little deeper into things with Mr. Henshaw. I don't suppose it was too pleasant for Derek when he had to own up to stealing, but I did get my job back. It was a kind thing for you to do."

"Good," said Sarah.

"But I can't do very much and I can't do it in front of an audience," said Anna.

Sarah frowned.

"Could you think of something I might do just for your science teacher—one small, unusual gesture to help you get a passing grade?" asked Anna.

Sarah looked very thoughtful. Then she grinned.

"Instead of doing something *for* my science teacher, could you do something *to* my science teacher?" she asked.

"It would depend," said Anna.

"Could you turn him into a frog?" asked Sarah.

"I think so," said Anna.

"That should be fine," said Sarah. "Just fine."

Sarah did not speak again after that. In fact no one spoke for a few minutes. Anna looked at Sarah and then at Ben questioningly.

"She's thinking," said Ben. "In fact, we may as well leave. I know Sarah. She's already figuring out how she can play this up for all it's worth. She won't be much fun until she gets it all worked out the way she wants."

"Ben's right," said Sarah, finishing off a last slice of banana bread. "I've got some thinking to do."

Anna walked with them to the front door. Ben looked around the living room once more as they passed through. It was a bright splash of air and color. A poster with a sun-stroked lake and rocks, paintings, and tapestries met in a gay dance on the walls. Throws of brilliant peacock blue covered the old sofa and chair. There was a large chest of polished wood before the front windows. Indian braided rugs patterned the floor. And everywhere, on shelves, in nooks and crannies and corners were small bright objects: carvings, candles, small porcelain bowls. Ben saw the painted box on a shelf at the end of the room.

"Would you like to look in it again?" asked Anna as Sarah walked out the door ahead of them.

"Yes," said Ben.

Anna passed him the box. Ben turned it in his hands. He was looking at the designs painted so carefully on the sides and lid.

"When I made the box, a long time ago, I painted on it all the small lovely things I remembered seeing as a child," said Anna.

"It's this one I especially like," said Ben. "The way you've painted it it looks like a butterfly with crystal wings."

Anna nodded.

Ben opened the box.

"1947 dot nickel!" he said with satisfaction.

He handed the box back to Anna and followed Sarah out the door.

*   *   *

"What happened out on the front steps?" asked Ben as he and Sarah walked home.

"It was the carving. I picked it up and suddenly became a bird without a tail about to wipe out at 500 mph," said Sarah. "Not fun." Then she thought a moment. "But before that . . . before that when the air currents were so strong they just held me up anyway, when I was soaring on the wind it was fine, really fine. Anastasia Morningstar has talent. Mr. Wyanth is going to be impressed. Really impressed. Once he gets over the shock of having webbed toes."

CHAPTER FIVE

The meeting between Anastasia Morningstar and Andrew Wyanth was arranged for Thursday afternoon, right after regular classes were over. Sarah walked into the classroom with Anastasia Morningstar behind her and Ben in the rear to close the door. Sarah wore her best, matter-of-fact manner.

"Hi, Mr. Wyanth," she said. "This is my science project."

Andrew Wyanth looked at Anastasia Morningstar. Anastasia Morningstar looked at Andrew Wyanth.

"Her name is Anastasia Morningstar," said Sarah. "She turns people into frogs."

"I see," said Mr. Wyanth, who had been expecting the worst and was apparently not going to be disappointed. "Nice to meet you, Miss Morningstar."

Anna said hello and the two of them shook hands.

"Before we do this," said Sarah, "I want to make sure everything is understood. If I have indeed produced a scientific phenomenon that can turn people into frogs, then, automatically, I pass my science project. No muss, no fuss, no questions asked."

Mr. Wyanth nodded.

"And if you haven't," he said, "you stop driving me nuts. You buckle down and act like a normal student for the rest of the year. That includes doing a regular science project."

"Right," said Sarah.

"I mean it, Sarah," said Mr. Wyanth. "Somehow I've got caught up in this odd little game of yours—but this *is* the end."

"All right, all right," said Sarah. "Ben is the judge."

"Ben is not the judge," said Mr. Wyanth. "I'm the judge."

"How can you be the judge? You're going to be a frog," said Sarah.

Mr. Wyanth gave Sarah his stormiest look.

Sarah perched up on the top of the nearest desk. Ben perched beside her.

"OK, Anna," said Sarah. "Do your stuff."

Anna walked up to Mr. Wyanth, reached out with one hand and touched him on the left shoulder.

"Frog," she said.

Mr. Wyanth remained Mr. Wyanth. Anastasia Morningstar remained Anastasia Morningstar. Sarah and Ben remained Sarah and Ben.

Sarah frowned and hopped off the desk.

"Just a moment," said Sarah to Mr. Wyanth. "My science project and I need to have a consultation."

Sarah whispered in Anna's ear. Anna nodded.

"Mr. Wyanth," said Sarah, taking him by the arm, "I think the light is wrong here. Over by the windows would be better. You look out at the street and I'll tell you when we're ready."

Sarah left him and jumped back on the desk. She nodded silently to Anna. Anna stepped quickly behind Mr. Wyanth and touched him on the left shoulder.

"Frog," she said.

Mr. Wyanth remained the same. Anna Morningstar remained the same. Ben and Sarah remained the same. Mr. Wyanth turned around to look at them questioningly.

Sarah frowned. No one said anything for what seemed like a long time. Then, abruptly, Sarah hopped off the desk.

"Never mind," she said. "Just a joke, Mr. Wyanth. See you in class tomorrow."

Without further explanation, Sarah turned and walked out the classroom door. Ben and Anna followed her. Sarah walked small and straight down the hall without looking behind her. She did not see Anna reach out and touch the few students at the lockers as she passed. Frog, bush, Grecian urn—they stood along the hall behind Sarah's small, tight back as she pushed out the heavy orange doors.

When she crossed the playground, Ben and Anna were still following her.

"Sarah," called Ben. "Sarah, wait up."

Sarah kept walking.

"Sarah!" called Ben.

She stood and turned.

"What do you want?" she asked.

"Wait up, that's all," said Ben.

"I can't wait," said Sarah. "I have to go buy two tons of macaroni so I can build the biggest, stupidest, dumbest, some-sort-of-science project ever."

"I'll help you," said Ben.

"I don't want help," said Sarah. "I don't need help. Not yours, or hers, or anybody's."

She turned and ran; across the playing field, over the fence with a well-timed jump, and across the street without looking back.

"She really, really wanted to turn Mr. Wyanth into a frog, you know," said Ben as he and Anna walked back toward Anna's house.

"I know," said Anna.

"I kind of wanted it to happen too," said Ben.

"Aren't you going to ask me what went wrong?" asked Anna.

"No," said Ben.

"Why not?" asked Anna.

"Because you don't know," said Ben. "Besides, what I really want to ask you is, why did you agree to help Sarah with her science project in the first place?"

"I owe her a favor for getting me my job back," said Anna. "Actually, I owe you both the favor."

"Maybe," said Ben. "But there's something else too. Something between you and Sarah. Something you're looking for."

Anna smiled, but did not answer.

"I don't think you are on the right track, though," said Ben. "There's nothing unusual about Sarah. I mean there's lots of unusual things about Sarah, but nothing like that."

"No," said Anna. "Nothing like that. But maybe it isn't necessary."

"What do you mean?" asked Ben.

"We can't talk now," said Anna.

They had turned onto Anna's street and both of them could see the hedge around her small, blue house.

"Instead of turning into my house up here, I think we'll just walk past it as if it's someone else's house. Then we'll go down another block and turn left. You can head back home. I'll double back a different way by myself," said Anna.

"What's wrong?" asked Ben.

"Someone's following us," said Anna. "And I don't particularly want to take him home with me."

She touched Ben's shoulder. It was just for a moment, but Ben could feel the presence of someone hovering near them; not too close but not too distant either. The person was sneaky and clever and had numerous other qualities that Ben felt as gently shaded textures.

"Derek Henshaw," said Ben. "What's he up to now!"

CHAPTER SIX

When Ben woke up the next morning, Grandpa Butler was sitting in a chair in the corner of the bedroom. He was asleep. A blanket was half-pulled around him and a pillow was propped between his head and the wall. Whenever Grandpa Butler had a nightmare, that was what he did. He went in and slept in one of the kids' rooms. It peeved Ben a bit. Grandpa Butler was the only person in the whole house who had a room of his own.

Ben dressed quickly and went out to the kitchen. He was the only one awake. He made himself a peanut butter sandwich and sat at the table. He was glad the house was quiet because he had to think. There was Sarah and there was Anastasia Morningstar and there was Derek Henshaw to think about. When he heard the baby waking up he put the coffee on for his mom and left a note saying he was going out for a walk.

Two hours later Sarah Mathews appeared in Ben Clark's kitchen. She arrived and sat in the corner

by the fridge for a full half hour before anyone, other than Ben's cousin (who had let her in on his way out), or the dogs (who seemed to assume if she hadn't rung the doorbell she'd been there all along and wasn't worth making a fuss about), knew she was there.

There were five people and two dogs in the Clark kitchen and all of them were talking at once, except the baby, who was crying. The kitchen table looked like a TV commercial for breakfast cereal gone mad. There were toys and cat food spilled all over the floor. The baby was spitting cereal across the room.

Ben's youngest sister was singing advertisements along with the radio. Grandpa Butler was reading aloud from the paper in fits and starts.

"Government brings in wage controls!" he roared. "They said they'd never do it. Never do it. But do the papers report that? No. Everyone forgets that. It's all new. All wonderful."

"Jamie, what's Tommy crying about?"

"He's on the pot."

"Can you go help him, please?"

"Now? Uck. No way. I'm eating. I'll chuck if I go now."

"Doctor," roared Grandpa Butler, "Doctor no less—*Doctor* Tanner Black, noted investigator of the supernatural, arrived in our city . . . they don't mention that he was here before, twenty years ago, he was known as Crazy Tanner, Used Car Salesman. People forget. People forget and the papers are in on it. It's all a conspiracy. What the heck. Used cars or the supernatural. It's all a flimflam salesman's job."

"Jamie, please. Tommy sounds desperate."

"I'll chuck. I can't do it. I'll chuck."

"I'll go," said Sarah.

Tommy was waiting for praise and assistance at the bathroom door. She helped him out and they both waved as they flushed it down the toilet. Then Tommy went racing off down the hall squealing Sarah's name at the top of his lungs.

After that Sarah would have liked to go and look for Ben herself but the first person she ran into was Ben's oldest brother coming down the hall smoking a cigarette with a towel wrapped around him. Somehow it didn't seem like the Ken she saw on the street in the daytime. It was strange being at someone else's house on a Saturday morning— strange at least in this part of the house where there were dark, quiet places and smells. Sarah opted for light and noise. She went back to the kitchen.

"Gold prices drop," read Grandpa Butler aloud. "I remember when they said the price of gold would never drop!"

A great howl cut him off.

"Somebody let the dog out!" called a voice from downstairs.

Two people ran to let the dog out. The dog went out. The cat came in. Tommy grabbed for it. It jumped from his arms onto the table, knocked over the cornflakes and fled down the hall.

"Who did that?" asked Ben's mom, turning to see the cornflakes in mid-air. Her eyes swept the room and stopped when they met Sarah's eyes.

"What are you doing here, Sarah?" she asked. "Were you looking for Ben?"

That was all she managed because the doorbell rang. Dog number two began to howl and everybody under the age of eight raced for the door. Grandpa Butler said in his loudest voice, "Someone's at the door."

Mike called from the other room. "Hey, mom, do you want to buy a vacuum cleaner?"

Sarah had to read Ben's mother's lips.

"He's not here," said the lips.

"Oh," said Sarah.

She left by the back door and went home.

Ben was sitting in Sarah's kitchen helping her mom with the Saturday crossword puzzle. It was so quiet Sarah could hear the sound of the pencil on the paper.

"Your place is a madhouse," said Sarah as they went downstairs.

"I know," said Ben. "It's enough to give an old man nightmares."

"Anyway, I figured it all out about yesterday. It was a bad case of overreaction on my part. I don't think she really meant to mess things up. I'm sorry I acted so stupid afterward."

"Good," said Ben. "Because there's a few things that I want to talk about with you."

"OK," said Sarah. "But let me finish with this

first. You see I came home and thought about it and thought about it. The problem is that I took the wrong approach. It's not Anastasia Morningstar I need for my science project. I don't even really need to turn Mr. Wyanth into anything. What I really need is her help in creating something truly unusual of my own. Something like this."

Sarah pointed toward a table on the far wall. On it sat a box with a glass top and front. Ben had seen it before. It was Sarah's old ant-colony box, but there was something changed about it. The tunnels were bigger, the rooms larger than before. In some of the corridors were tiny ball bearings and pieces of large plastic drinking straws. In one of the rooms was a very small stick balanced across a tiny round

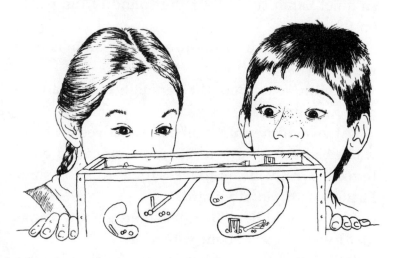

tube. Some of the other things, Ben couldn't even hope to recognize, but on the surface of the colony he thought he saw something that looked like the world's most miniature swing set.

"Do you know what it is?" asked Sarah.

"I've got a pretty good idea," said Ben.

"It's not Disneyland, but there's a certain appeal to it, don't you think?" asked Sarah. And she set the miniature swing in motion.

CHAPTER SEVEN

Anna's house, that Saturday afternoon, was full of air and sunlight. All the windows were open to the outdoors and all the drapes were pulled as far back as possible. Anna herself was replacing several worn squares of tile around the stove. She had managed to rip them all out when Sarah and Ben arrived.

"I want you to turn me into an ant," said Sarah.

"It's been done before," said Anna. "To tell you the truth, the scientific data on ants is quite thorough and quite accurate."

"I don't want to study them, I want to change them," said Sarah. "Mr. Wyanth is always talking about how hard ants work: building, moving, tunnelling. I want to introduce them to a new way of life."

"I don't think it will work. They don't exactly have minds like ours, you know," said Anna.

"I'd like to try," said Sarah. "I can be quite persuasive. Are there any ants in your garden?"

"Yes," said Anna.

"Good," said Sarah. "Let's go."

In the backyard, Sarah chose ten healthy-looking ants and put them in the colony box. She put in a piece of fruit and some pieces of bread smeared with peanut butter. Anna and she decided upon a series of simple maneuvers for her to perform when she wanted to get out of the box and become Sarah again. Then Anna changed her into an ant. Sarah walked into the box.

"This could take a bit of time," said Anna to Ben. "I've more work to do inside. Do you want to come with me?"

"Do you think it's safe to leave her alone?" asked Ben.

"Yes," said Anna. "It'll be all right. I've given her a certain amount of protection."

Ben looked at the box.

"I think I'll stay anyway," he said and sat down on the lawn nearby.

It was not particularly interesting watching the box. As far as Ben could tell it was just a bunch of ants milling around. He couldn't even be sure which one was Sarah, although every once in a while one of the ants would actually begin to swing and he thought that was probably Sarah, but he didn't know for sure. Anna came out several times to check things out. Each time she was rather sur-

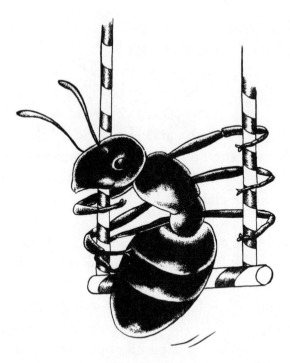

prised that Sarah had not given up, but she seemed
to know what was happening and who was Sarah.
Finally, she and Ben went around to the back porch
and sat and drank iced tea.

It was as Ben and Anna were sitting there that
Ben looked up and saw the butterfly resting beneath the eaves. At first he thought it only odd that
a butterfly would be resting in the shade when they
were usually drawn by the sun's heat to feed on
the flowers at this time of day. And then he began
to look at it. There was no color in its wings. They
looked like slightly clouded glass.

"The crystal butterfly," said Ben. "Like the one painted on your box."

Anna nodded.

"It has been here for two weeks now. I brought it under the eaves because I was afraid the birds might find it. When it first arrived it was like air, or ice. It was exactly the way I remembered seeing it as a child. Then it began to change and I remembered the poem."

"What poem?" asked Ben.

Anna looked up at the butterfly. She said the words in the same way Ben's little brother might roll off a nursery rhyme.

But when the light begins with age
To dull and wax upon its wings,
One will come with spirit strong
Therein light of renewal sings.
In search of sun and wind and sky
Three shall gather, high on high,
To free the crystal butterfly.

"But if it's a butterfly, it lays eggs and then there is a caterpillar and then a chrysalis and then a butterfly again," said Ben.

"That would work if there were two of them," said Anna. "But there's only one. It renews itself some other way. In fact, when you see it—clear and breathlessly alive—it seems more like a perfect thought than a living thing."

"But when the light begins with age to dull and wax upon its wings, one will come with spirit strong . . ." repeated Ben. He looked at Anna. "Sarah!" he said.

"I don't know," said Anna. "The truth is, I didn't even believe in the poem at first. It's just a scrap of a poem and I don't really know where it came from. I've known it all my life, I suppose. A lot of that type of thing means nothing at all. Then you and Sarah showed up. I don't know," Anna smiled. "Maybe I only used an old poem as an excuse to make friends."

"What is the rest of it again?" asked Ben.

In search of sun and wind and sky
Three shall gather, high on high,
To free the crystal butterfly.

"I don't know what it means, so don't ask me," said Anna.

"When are you going to tell Sarah about it?" asked Ben.

"I'm not," said Anna. "And neither are you. I don't believe in hocus-pocus. If it happens, it happens. If it doesn't—if the butterfly has merely come here to die in peace as the last of its kind—I don't want Sarah thinking it's her fault. All right?"

Ben nodded.

"But you wanted to see if Sarah knew about it. That's why you gave her the box," said Ben.

"Partly," said Anna. "Few things we do are as simple as they seem."

Sarah came around the corner of the house. Her hair was frazzled and her clothes were filthy. She was a mess.

"It's useless," she said, flopping down on the steps beside Ben. "You can't teach ants anything. Strictly robotic."

"Sarah," said Ben. "Have you ever seen a butterfly like that one up there before?"

Sarah glanced up.

"Nope," she said. "Come on. Let's go home."

"It's quite an unusual butterfly," said Ben.

"Butterfly, schmutterfly. I've had it with insects," said Sarah. "Thanks anyway, Anna. Catch you later. Come on, Ben. Let's go home."

On the way home, Sarah and Ben stopped at the store and bought two cherry slushes. Sarah seemed to feel a good bit better after that.

"I'm not giving up yet," she said as she sipped slowly on the cold, sweet slush.

"I don't think Anna expects you to," said Ben.

"Then why doesn't she help me, Ben?" asked Sarah with a frown. "I mean, she does what I ask, or tries to, but she doesn't really help. She doesn't tell us anything about herself or what she can do. Unless . . . has she been talking to you?"

"What she's said has to do more with you than with her, actually," began Ben.

"Then I'd just as soon not hear it," said Sarah. "I've been going off in all the wrong directions so far. I think she'll give me another chance, but this time it has got to be something a little more controlled. Spectacular, but controlled."

"Maybe the science project isn't really that important," said Ben.

"It's not the project itself, exactly, anymore," said Sarah. "It's the principle of the thing. It's how I am and how Mr. Wyanth is and it's something else, too. I'm missing my big chance. I know I am. I can feel it."

CHAPTER EIGHT

Tanner Black had taken a room on the twenty-third floor of the Holiday Inn downtown. From its window he could look across the entire west end of the city where he had got his start in life. More important, he could look down upon the corner of Eighth and Huron where "Crazy Tanner's Used Car Lot" had stood twenty years earlier.

Selling used cars, he thought to himself, as he had many times before, really wasn't very different from selling the supernatural. A salesman was a salesman. Instead of selling '57 Chevies he was selling subscriptions to *Supernatural Life Magazine* and memberships in "Supernatural Research Incorporated." In both cases the product was something about which people were skeptical on the surface but in which, deep down, they really wanted to believe. By switching to the supernatural, however, he had gained a reputation and stature of which he was very fond. He was looked upon as a man of intelligence and education. He liked that.

Tanner Black looked out across the west end and smiled. Then he turned around and looked sternly at the young man who was sitting on the chair behind him.

"Well, son, what have you got for me?" he asked. "And remember I'm not interested in fairy stories. I've heard too many of them not to smell them out for what they are."

"No, sir," said the boy. "That is, yes, sir. That is, I think you'll like this, sir."

He handed across a brown envelope. Tanner

Black nodded approvingly. He much preferred all the information presented this way, instead of someone rattling on for hours about pictures that fell off the wall and doors that wouldn't open. He was in need of a find just now. He needed something fresh to generate interest and contributions. He opened the envelope and looked briefly through several sheets of paper. Then he came to a small snapshot. He looked at it for several minutes. He knew the face. This was the fourth time in as many years that the same face had come forward.

"Is this woman still in town?" he asked.

"Oh, yes, sir," said the boy.

"Are you sure?" he asked.

"Yes."

"And does she know you're interested in her?"

"No," said the boy. "I've been careful about that."

Tanner Black smiled expansively and held out his hand to the boy.

"Well, my friend, I think we can do business together. What did you say your name was?"

"Derek Henshaw," the boy replied.

*   *   *

Andrew Wyanth loved science. He loved the purity of it and he loved the exactitude of it. He loved it because every time a piece of litmus paper turned from red to blue, or a seed sprouted, or Venus appeared as the evening star exactly where it should in the dusk sky, the laws of nature were affirmed.

Anastasia Morningstar intrigued him more than he liked to admit. He knew that she, Sarah, and Ben were still friends. He could tell by the questions Sarah asked all week in class. They were questions about the fantastic, the unknown, the unexpected. When he happened to mention the old alchemists' quest for a method of transmutation of metal, from iron to gold, her eyes lit up anew. After class Sarah and Ben stayed behind to talk with him about it.

"I suppose if something like that were discovered today it would wreak havoc with the stock market and completely mess up the international monetary exchange," said Sarah.

"Yes, I think you've pretty well described what would happen," said Mr. Wyanth.

"Too bad," said Sarah.

"How's your moonscape coming, Ben?" asked Mr. Wyanth.

"Pretty good," said Ben. "Thanks for getting me those maps from the space research center."

"You're welcome," said Mr. Wyanth. "Are you still working on a project with your friend, Sarah?"

Sarah nodded.

"We're going over there tonight. She said she had something she wanted to show us."

"Does she live around here then?" asked Mr. Wyanth.

"Over on Twenty-third Street," said Sarah. "Why?"

"I don't know," answered Mr. Wyanth truthfully.

Even after supper that evening, as he stopped his car in front of the house on Twenty-third Street, he couldn't truthfully say he knew exactly why he was there. He knew it was the right house. He had looked up the address in the phone book, but even without that assurance the small blue house with the shutters and latticed windows simply felt right. And he knew it was the right house because, as he was beside the doorstep, planning how he was going to begin his conversation with Anastasia Morningstar, Sarah and Ben themselves came around the hedge and through the gate and up to the door past him.

"What are you doing here?" asked Ben. "Did she invite you too?"

"No," said Mr. Wyanth.

"Then what are you doing here?" asked Sarah.

There was no time to answer. At the sound of Sarah's voice the door before them opened. A warm, sweet wind rushed out to meet them.

"That's odd," said Ben.

"Anna! Hello, Anna!" called Sarah. She looked

through the door. "Ben!" she said.

Ben peered through the doorway beside her.

"Holy-Mo—" he said.

They both stepped inside.

Inside the house was a small lake, sparkling and sunstroked. Its shores were beaded with tiny, water-smoothed pebbles. Around the lake stretched a meadow of bright flowers. At some distance to them the sun glanced off an immense ridge of white and golden rocks. On the far left was a forest of tall trees with needles as pale and intricate as lace. About it all there was a high, airy feeling— as if they were in some alpine meadow close to the very top of the world itself.

"Have you found her yet?"

Anna walked out of the lacy trees in a dress as green and delicate as the forest itself. Her hair hung long and flowing around her. Her eyes were dark and beautiful and sparkled with a secret too good to keep.

"Found who?" asked Sarah.

"The dragon," said Anna.

"No," said Sarah.

"You will," said Anna. "I never knew myself, until several days ago, that she was in the poster at all."

"How big a dragon?" asked Ben.

"How big do they come?" asked Anna.

No one answered this question for at that moment the row of gold and white rocks undulated and rolled. From out of the meadow flowers rose a great gold and silver head with bright, red-jeweled eyes. The eyes looked at Ben and Sarah and Anna. They blinked twice. Then the entire great body rolled onto its back and lay among the flowers, basking in the warmth of the sun.

Anna laughed with such clear amusement that Ben and Sarah found they were grinning too.

"Come," said Anna. "She talked to me yesterday. She only needs to be coaxed awake a bit."

She drew back her hair and turned with childlike anticipation and that was when she saw Andrew Wyanth appearing in the door. Both Sarah and Ben had forgotten about him but as soon as they saw Anna's face they knew instantly what was wrong. She stood looking at him for perhaps thirty seconds. All around the room was deathly quiet.

Then it was gone: the lake, the meadow, the dragon itself. Gone like the turning of a page in a book.

On the far side of the room Ben and Sarah found themselves looking at one of Anna's posters where a picture showed a small sun-stroked lake in a field of flowers and rocks.

Anna was not looking at the poster. She was looking at Andrew Wyanth. Not since she was a very small child playing games that no one else could ever believe, had she been caught so far from cover, so vulnerable.

Andrew Wyanth crossed the room and stood before her. His face was dark and demanding.

"Who are you?" he asked, his voice hard. "What are you?"

Anna looked directly back at him, but there was fear in her voice, a kind of pain.

"I am Anastasia Morningstar," she said.

"That's no answer," said Mr. Wyanth. He was angry the way people are angry when they have to reach too far for something they should not have to try to understand. "I want to know. Who are you!"

"I am Anastasia Morningstar," said Anna. "It's all the answer I have."

She ran, sweeping past Andrew Wyanth and out the open door. Mr. Wyanth turned to follow her. Ben tripped him. Sarah threw the cover from the sofa over his head. Sarah and Ben raced after Anna. She was well past the end of the block when they caught up with her.

"I'm sorry," said Sarah. "I'm sorry. It's my fault he was there. I didn't bring him but he knew we were coming to see you. He was just there when we came. But I didn't bring him on purpose. You have to believe me. I didn't understand before, about you. I was thinking about me and how great I was going to be and I didn't understand, but I still didn't bring him. Anna!"

Anna stopped and turned and looked at the worried faces of Ben and Sarah.

"I didn't bring him," said Sarah.

"No," said Anna. "Of course you didn't!"

She reached out and took both Ben and Sarah by the hand. The three of them walked the last block and crossed to the grass of the park. When they reached the hollow well away from the road, Anna said, "Hold tight," and then she said, "tree."

Together they grew tall on tall with the sun and wind in their leaves and their roots deep in the earth. The limits of the human world receded far behind the simple wonder of life itself.

CHAPTER NINE

"'**B**ut why do you have to leave?" asked Sarah. "Why can't you wait and see what happens? Maybe Mr. Wyanth won't do anything. Maybe he'll think he imagined the whole thing. Maybe he'll think he's crazy and move to the south pole."

Sarah and Ben had stopped at Anna's house after school. It was two days later. The house was full of boxes, most of them already filled. Anna was packing dishes in the kitchen. She shook her head as she answered.

"A person can let almost anything slip by him, if it's small and if it only happens once. That's how I get away with turning people into frogs. But your Mr. Wyanth saw too much."

"He's not our Mr. Wyanth," said Sarah. "He's not anybody's Mr. Wyanth. He's just a dumb science teacher who has no imagination."

"Perhaps," said Anna. "In any case, he's not the main problem. This is the main problem."

She took a book from the counter and handed it

to Ben. Ben knew the feeling. It was the same feeling he had found out about the day they had been followed.

"Derek Henshaw," said Ben. "And somebody else. Somebody who gives me the creeps."

"What are you talking about?" asked Sarah.

Ben handed her the book. She weighed it in her hands. It felt like a book.

Anna placed her hand on Sarah's shoulder.

"Oh," said Sarah.

"I only noticed it this morning when I was moving some things around. It was two days ago they were here, I think. They must have come in the evening Mr. Wyanth was here and the house was left open to the winds."

"Who was with Derek?" asked Ben. "Do you know?"

"I know," said Anna. "His name is Tanner Black. He 'investigates' the supernatural, the occult. He doesn't differentiate between the genuine or the fake, between people who want to belong to the occult and people who are just . . . different. He deals in sensationalism and publicity and money. He knows me already. He wants me."

"What do you mean he wants you?" asked Sarah.

"I'm to be the next 'Mistress of Black Magic' for his magazine. The next evil to be investigated, and probably purged, for a price. It's all a bunch of rot but too many people will believe him. Too many people believe in him already."

"So you're running away," said Sarah.

"I'm not running away," said Anna. "I'm leaving. I'm going elsewhere."

"Same thing," said Sarah.

"I'm not running away from myself," said Anna. "I know perfectly well who I am and I like it. If I want to keep on being me, this is the only way."

"You could fight him," said Sarah.

"I can't fight anyone," said Anna. "I'm not . . . I'm not like other people. The same rules don't seem to apply to me, or for me."

"You could fight him on your own terms," said Sarah. "You could turn him into something. It could be something permanent. A monument. A slab of sidewalk."

"No," said Anna. "I don't do things that way. The only solution is for me to leave. I've had to do it many times before, for many reasons, and I'll have to do it many times again. My life is different from yours. I've known that for a long time."

"Why don't you just turn yourself into a fly and stay here until things cool down," suggested Ben.

"I don't like being a fly," said Anna.

"Well, then turn yourself into a tree. Plant yourself in your own yard. Be a bird, or rain, or last year's carrots out in the garden," said Sarah.

Anna put one arm around Ben and one arm around Sarah.

"There's one thing you're not taking into account with all your plans, you two. I like being me. I like living the way I do and doing the things I do. I like being Anastasia Morningstar—just the way I am."

"But you don't like leaving," said Sarah.

"No," said Anna quietly. "I never do like the leaving."

Sarah stood up and went into the living room. She sat on the scatter rug. She was thinking. Very hard.

"What about your friend?" asked Ben.

He and Anna went to the back door and looked beneath the eaves. The butterfly rested there motionless. Ben had seen it change slowly over the past days. Its wings were no longer merely clouded, they were heavy and waxen, the scales curling. Its body was thickened and dull gray.

"It won't even come to me," said Anna. "You try, Ben."

Ben climbed up on the railing. He reached out his hand. He drew his fingers slowly close beside the waxen butterfly. It moved away with an odd rocking motion. "Will you take it with you?" asked Ben.

Anna shook her head.

"There isn't much time left now. For that short time, at least, I must stay."

Sarah came out the back door. She glanced up at the butterfly and frowned, but her mind was on other things.

"You're in charge of talking to Mr. Wyanth," said Sarah when they had left Anna's house. "You're bound to have better luck at that than I am."

"What are you going to do?" asked Ben.

"I'm going to the library. I think there was something about Tanner Black in the paper last week. I've also been thinking about how there used to be people hired to go around hunting out witches. I don't know. Maybe if I read about them I'd get some sort of an idea about what we could do," said Sarah.

"Maybe," said Ben.

Sarah looked at him.

"I hope so," said Sarah, "because most of this is my fault. If I hadn't started getting carried away with my science project Anna would have just got another job and Derek would have forgotten about her, and Tanner Black and Mr. Wyanth wouldn't have known about her at all."

"I don't think Anna blames you," said Ben.

"I blame me," said Sarah. "And I'm going to fix things. All I need is a decent plan."

Andrew Wyanth had not slept for two days. He was worried that he was losing his mind. He was worried that he wasn't losing his mind. He was worried because he should have already done something about Anastasia Morningstar and he hadn't. For days he had taught his classes and fed his animals as if nothing unusual was happening. It was a relief when Ben came to him at last.

"Mr. Wyanth," said Ben. "I'm afraid I'm running into a bit of trouble with my moonscape. Could I have an extra week?"

"No," said Mr. Wyanth.

"OK," said Ben.

"Anything else?" asked Mr. Wyanth.

"About Anastasia Morningstar," began Ben.

"Well, what about her?"

"What do you think about her and about what happened the other night?" asked Ben.

Mr. Wyanth took a long time before answering. Even then he didn't say what he meant to say.

"Was she the one who gave you the box?" he asked instead. "The box with the butterfly inside?"

Ben smiled.

"Yes," said Ben. "The way it worked was that everybody saw something different in it. They saw something they had had, and then lost. Sarah saw a robin's egg. I saw a 1947 dot nickel. You're the only one who saw a butterfly."

"I didn't just see a butterfly," said Andrew Wyanth. "I saw . . . that is, I thought I saw . . . a living butterfly with crystal wings. How could I have seen that before? Except I had the oddest feeling . . ."

". . . that you had!" said Ben.

Mr. Wyanth rose and looked out the window across the playground. There are, in everybody's memory, things that hover just out of reach. There are things so real one can feel them waiting there, but if one tries to touch them they slide quickly beyond one's grasp and vanish: the crystal butterfly.

"It doesn't change things," said Mr. Wyanth. "I'm a teacher. I'm responsible for the well-being of the children of my class. There are things about Anastasia Morningstar for which I can't find any explanation. It's probably going to mean that you and Sarah won't be able to have quite the same . . . relationship . . . with her that you've been having."

"We're friends," said Ben.

Mr. Wyanth turned and looked at Ben. For the first time Ben realized how tired and drawn his face was.

"I know," said Mr. Wyanth. "But there are things that don't make any sense. . . ."

"Everything doesn't have to make sense among friends," said Ben.

"Some things *have* to make sense. . . ." said Mr. Wyanth.

"And there is a crystal butterfly," said Ben. "Now. At Anna's house. And it's dying."

Andrew Wyanth shook his head.

"No, Ben," he said. "Go home."

* * *

"How did you make out?" Sarah asked that evening as they sat on the back steps of her house.

"I didn't," said Ben. "He won't give it a chance. It makes me mad because part of him understands somehow. I know it does, but it's not the part that he is going to listen to. He's going to tell someone something, not the truth but some scientifically scrambled rationalization that will make Anna look bad. The school board, maybe even the police . . ."

"Tanner Black," said Sarah.

"Tanner Black is sure to hear about it," said Ben. "It will be one more piece of information for him to use. 'Sorceress leads youth cult in worship of dragons.' What did you find out, Sarah?"

"Nothing," said Sarah. "That is, I found a lot of hocus-pocus, as Anna calls it, about pins and dunkings and the full moon. But none of it fits. Anna's not a witch and Tanner Black's not an eighteenth century witch hunter. Tanner Black doesn't need needles and birthmarks. He knows how to use the press."

It was very quiet in Sarah's backyard. The shadow from the garage lengthened to cover the garden. Somewhere down the block two children began the rhythmic repetition of a skipping song.

"What I don't understand is," said Sarah, "if she's going to leave like she says, why is she still here? Why doesn't she just leave and get it over with? It's as if she's waiting for something."

"She is," said Ben."

"Well then, what is it?" asked Sarah.

Ben took a deep breath before answering.

"She's waiting for the butterfly."

CHAPTER TEN

Even before Ben opened his eyes the next morning he knew Grandpa Butler was back in the bedroom. He could feel him there. And as he lay in the gray light of dawn, he heard the snoring begin again.

Ben slid out of bed and dressed quietly. In the kitchen his mother was up feeding the baby.

"'Did Grandpa sleep in your room again last night?" she asked Ben.

"Yes," said Ben. "Why does he do that? He's the only one in the whole house with a room of his own."

"When he was young, he used to sleep in a room with five other brothers," said Ben's mom.

"Good for him," said Ben. "It's time he grew up."

Ben's mother looked at Ben and then at the baby and then at Ben again.

"Sometimes it's not easy being Grandpa Butler," she said. "Just like sometimes it's not easy being Ben Clark."

Ben folded his peanut butter sandwich in half

and sat down at the table. His mother was not Anastasia Morningstar, but she too could feel things sometimes.

"I told something to Sarah that I wasn't supposed to tell. I only did it because I thought it would help. Now I'm not so sure," he said.

"Are you going over there now?" asked his mom.

Ben nodded.

"I can't help, can I?" she asked.

"No," said Ben. "But thanks."

He found Sarah sitting on her back porch waiting for him.

"I'm going to save the butterfly," she said.

"Sarah . . ." Ben began.

"I know, I know. You explained it all yesterday about how I'm probably not the one at all and about how it's probably just the last of its kind, a freak of nature whose time has come, how even Anna didn't really believe the poem and doesn't still. But I've got it figured out."

Ben sat down on the steps beside her and put his head in his hands.

"You look awful," said Sarah. "I hope you didn't stay up all night worrying about everything."

Ben shook his head.

"It's Grandpa. Whenever he can't sleep he gets up and comes into the room with Josh and me and props himself up in a chair. I guess he just wants

to be near someone. But he snores. And wheezes.
And last night he held long conversations with all
my great-aunts and -uncles."

"I kind of like your Grandpa Butler," said Sarah.
"When I was at your place the other day he was
reading aloud from the paper. No one was listening
but he was reading anyway."

"And saying how nobody remembers," said Ben.

"Right. Nobody remembers political promises. Nobody remembers the price of gold. Nobody remembers Tanner Black was Crazy Tanner. Sometimes I wish there was someone to do something like that at my house. I mean my mom's exactly the way she's supposed to be, but things would be pretty dull around here if it wasn't for me," said Sarah.

"Was Tanner Black really Crazy Tanner?" asked Ben. "Even my dad mentioned what a crook Crazy Tanner used to be."

"I don't know," said Sarah. "That's what your Grandpa said. Maybe he has him mixed up with someone else. I don't know how he'd know for sure."

"He *could* know," said Ben. "Grandpa used to work for one of the banks downtown. If Crazy Tanner had dealt at that bank, Grandpa would have known his real name."

"But the newspapers didn't say anything about Crazy Tanner," said Sarah thoughtfully.

"Maybe *they* don't know," said Ben. "I mean Grandpa always calls things like that a great conspiracy, but maybe no one down there has ever made the connection."

"And Tanner Black isn't telling them," said Sarah.

"It wouldn't exactly be good publicity," said Ben.

"It would be lousy publicity for someone in Dr. Tanner Black's position," said Sarah. "If he was such a crook back then, it might even be more than bad publicity." Sarah jumped up. "Come on, Ben. We might not be on the right track but it's the only thing I can think of. If we catch the right buses, we can be downtown in no time."

"We should tell Anna first," said Ben.

"We'll phone her from the newspaper," said Sarah. "Let's go. The sooner we get going on this, the sooner we'll know if there's anything in it."

*   *   *

The newspaper office, in a big new building downtown, was bright and busy. Sarah had been directed to a junior reporter but she walked right past him as if he wasn't there and walked to a glass door marked EDITOR and went inside.

The editor was a short-tempered man who regularly threw adults bodily out of his office. Throwing children bodily around, however, is not allowed, so he had to listen to Sarah.

"Your paper has run a couple of articles on Dr. Tanner Black, investigator of the occult," said Sarah.

"Well?" said the editor.

"Well," said Sarah. "We thought it might lend a better balance to your articles if you also mentioned that twenty years ago he went by the name of Crazy

Tanner and ran a place called 'Crazy Tanner's Carz' on the west side of town."

"You weren't even alive twenty years ago," said the editor with a frown. Then he began to tap his pen on the telephone thoughtfully. "But there was this place down in the west end run by a two-bit con man when I first moved here. Crazy something, all right." He scowled at Sarah and Ben. "Wait outside," he said abruptly.

Sarah and Ben waited outside. Through the window they watched the editor dial, speak briefly on the phone and hang up. Then he dialed again. The conversation this time was a bit longer, but not much. He opened the door and stuck his head out.

"It's him all right," he told Sarah and Ben.

"How did you find out for sure?" asked Ben.

"I phoned him and asked him," said the editor. "Got the oddest response—something between a maybe, positively not, no comment, are you from the police, type of answer. I told him I'd send a reporter around this afternoon to get his side of the story. On second thought, could I send someone right away? I think I rattled the poor man more than I meant to. I don't want him fading out of town before we get a chance to take a closer look."

The editor's lip lifted slightly in what was almost a smile. Then he slammed the door and went back to his desk.

Ben phoned Anna's house from a pay phone outside the newspaper office.

"What did she say?" asked Sarah after he had hung up.

"She was surprised," said Ben. "She didn't really know what to say but she laughed when I told her about the editor. It's a good thing I phoned, though. She was getting ready to leave."

"The butterfly," said Sarah.

"I think so," said Ben. "Look. Let's run the six blocks over to Fourth Street and see if we can't catch a blue arrow bus.

Even before he had finished the sentence, they were both running.

*   *   *

Andrew Wyanth and Anastasia Morningstar were sitting on the back porch when Sarah and Ben got to Anna's house. In the palm of Mr. Wyanth's hand was the butterfly. Its body and wings were thick, heavy, waxen, and unmoving.

"Mr. Wyanth. What are you doing here?" asked Sarah.

"I came to see something I'd been told about," he answered, looking at Ben. "Something I still can't explain. Something I'd seen before but couldn't quite admit to."

"Do you think you can save it?" asked Sarah.

"I wish I could," he said.

"I can," said Sarah.

She took the butterfly from his hand and carried it into the house on her own hand. Ben heard the door lock behind her.

"I'm sorry," said Ben to Anna. "I told her."

"It's all right," said Anna.

"But she's gone ahead and started acting just like you were afraid she would. She never does anything halfway, or slowly, or bit by bit. She always walks right in there like she owns the whole world."

"That's why she's your friend," said Anna.

Ben sighed and sat on the steps.

"You should have seen her at the paper. We wouldn't have got past the front desk if it wasn't for Sarah. I don't know exactly what background they'll find to print in the afternoon edition, but I don't think it will please Dr. Tanner Black," said Ben.

"Tanner Black?" asked Mr. Wyanth.

"Alias Crazy Tanner," said Ben.

"Alias witch hunter," said Anna.

Ben and Andrew Wyanth both turned toward Anna.

"Don't look at me," she said. "I don't believe in witches either."

"Did you really see the butterfly a long time ago?" Ben asked.

Mr. Wyanth nodded.

"When I was very, very young, but I've never really forgotten about it. It filled me with a sense of wonder. I think, in a way it was what made me look at things more closely. It was what made me interested in science."

"And is that why you couldn't change him into a frog the other day?" Ben asked Anna. "Something to do with the butterfly?"

"I think so," said Anna. "I don't really understand it. He certainly seems to be quite immune."

Ben looked at Mr. Wyanth, and then at Anna, and then back again.

"Can you . . . that is, do you . . . ?" he began.

"Can I do the things Anastasia Morningstar can do?" asked Mr. Wyanth.

Ben nodded.

"No," said Mr. Wyanth. He smiled and shook his head. "I tried a few things earlier and, no, I can't. Immunity seems to be my only talent." He glanced sideways at Anna. "A talent which I am in no way underestimating."

"At least you can stay now," said Ben.

"Yes," said Anna, but Ben had caught her glancing over her shoulder and he knew she was thinking about other things.

*   *   *

At last the back door opened and Sarah came

back out. She was carrying a brown paper bag. She sat down on the back steps also.

"Well, Mr. Wyanth. I've thought of something to do for my science project. Have you and Anna come to some sort of an understanding about who she is?"

"I think so," said Mr. Wyanth.

"Good," said Sarah. "You can go home now."

"I beg your pardon?"

"You can go home now. Good-bye. See you Monday. The science fair's next week, you know. I bet you have a lot of work to do between now and then."

"Sarah, what's wrong?" asked Anna. "If it's the butterfly . . . don't. It's I who've failed it, not you."

"Nobody failed anybody," said Sarah. "It's just that the poem says, 'And three shall gather high on high.' Three. Mr. Wyanth makes four and he's holding things up. And, if we really wanted to do this with class, we should find a mountain to climb."

"Sarah!" said Anna softly.

"OK, OK. Let's try it this way," said Sarah. "Mr. Wyanth, you go and sit down on the grass. Ben and Anna and I will sit here on the steps. That's hardly high on high but maybe it will be OK."

Mr. Wyanth sighed. He stood up from the steps,

crossed to an old stump beside the flower beds, and sat down again.

"Do you think I should say some magic words for effect?" Sarah asked Anna.

Anna shook her head. She was looking at the bag.

Sarah shrugged good-naturedly and opened the top of the bag.

"OK, butterfly," she said. "Take off."

At first nothing happened. Then there was a small, pathetic scratching sound at the bottom of the bag. Sarah peered inside and frowned. She held the bag at a gentle angle. There were a few more scratching sounds and then the crystal butterfly climbed onto the rim of the bag. Its body was like clearest water. Its wings were like glass or ice. Its existence was marked only by the reflection and refraction of light itself.

It stood on the rim of the bag. Its wings moved in the air, but it was a helpless, feeble motion.

"It can't fly," said Sarah. Her voice was very soft but Ben could feel the despair rising within. "It can't fly!"

"Wait," said Mr. Wyanth. He had come close and was observing the butterfly. "Give it time. The new wings of a butterfly, perhaps even a butterfly such as this, need time to harden with the air. Give it time."

Sarah set her lips tightly. The four of them watched the scrap of light, the slender slice of imagination and, for those moments at least, it seemed to each of them that all things were possible.

The movements of the butterfly's wings became stronger. At last it rose on the air. It tested its wings in two small spirals beside the house. Then it began to rise on the air currents. Higher and higher it sailed, a bare turning of light in the air and gone.

*   *   *

Sarah Mathews' science project that year was a

large needle, a doll that had been bound hands and heels and was sunk in a pail of water, and a picture of a birthmark. It wasn't particularly impressive to look at but Mr. Wyanth gave her a B+ for the vividness with which she described the ancient tests for witches and the scientific reasons why they produced unexpected results.

Ben got his usual A for his macaroni moonscape done in painstaking detail. He brought Grandpa Butler with him to the science fair for the day. Grandpa Butler and Anastasia Morningstar hit it off right away. They toured all the projects with great enthusiasm. Even afterward Ben couldn't quite figure out whether it was Grandpa Butler or Anna who got Derek Henshaw's mouse to run the maze correctly after it had persisted in climbing over the barricades all morning. He only knew that Derek Henshaw was pleased afterward and on better terms with both Anna and Ben himself.

The crystal butterfly was not seen again that summer in Anna's garden. It remained a quiet secret among Anna, Ben, Sarah, and Andrew Wyanth. Sarah did, however, explain her part in it to Ben.

"I used a kitchen knife," she told him.

"A kitchen knife!" said Ben.

"Right," said Sarah. "To open up the shell. That's all the wax stuff was. It wasn't living anymore. The new butterfly was trapped inside. That's what the poem meant. 'Therein light of renewal sings, in search of sun and wind and sky.' I don't know why everybody else didn't figure it out. It was as if you were all looking for some sort of magical potion or person or something. Anyway, all the butterfly needed was a little help getting out."

"So you took a kitchen knife to it!" said Ben.

"There wasn't time to be fancy," said Sarah. "Do you think we'll ever see it again?"

"I don't know," said Ben. "Somehow I don't think part of it, the idea of it at least, is ever very far from Anna."

"I know what you mean," said Sarah. She sat a moment, trying to put something she was feeling into words. Then she gave up and turned to practical things.

"It's hot. Let's go buy a slush," she said. "My treat."